Written by
Lou John

Illustrated by
Jenny Bloomfield

THE WORRY JAR

OXFORD
UNIVERSITY PRESS

Frida worried every day.
Big worries,
little worries,
all-the-time worries.

Her worries felt heavy, just like
the pebbles she collected.

Frida picked up pebbles
everywhere she went —
one for every worry.

Before school, Frida worried about the weather.

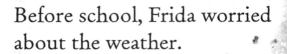

Would it rain?

Or maybe it would be too sunny?

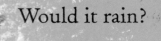

Should she wear her wellies or her sunhat?

Frida decided to wear both, just in case.

Then she worried that she might have forgotten to pack everything in her bag.

She triple checked, just to make sure.

On the way to school, Frida stopped to pick up another pebble and popped it in her pocket.

At school, Frida worried about where to sit.

There was a space on Milo's table and one on Pip's.

But Frida didn't want either of them to feel left out so she went off to read her book.

At playtime, Frida wanted to go on the slide,
but she was worried it might be too fast.

She decided to watch instead and that's
when she spotted a very special pebble.

It was shiny
and black
and it glinted in the sunlight.

She picked it up.

After school, Frida went to Milo's house for tea.

But at teatime she worried about the peas.

They were very green and they rolled around a lot.

At bedtime, Frida couldn't find Rabbit.

She was worried that she wouldn't sleep without him.

So she got into bed, slipped
her hand under the pillow, and
gently stroked her special pebble.

The pebble was warm and smooth.
Maybe she *would* be fine without
Rabbit after all?

On Saturday, it was swim club.

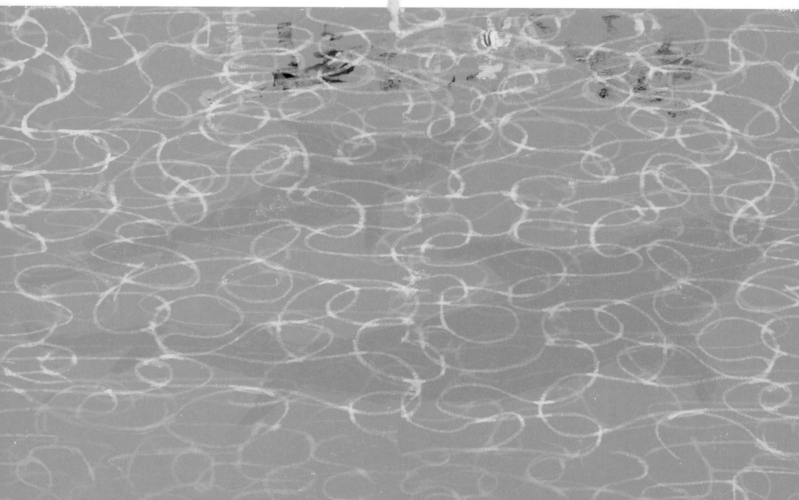

Frida worried that the water might be too deep.
She worried that she might have forgotten how to swim or that
there might be a shark lurking under the calm blue surface!

'Jump in!' said Milo,
'you can swim like a fish!'

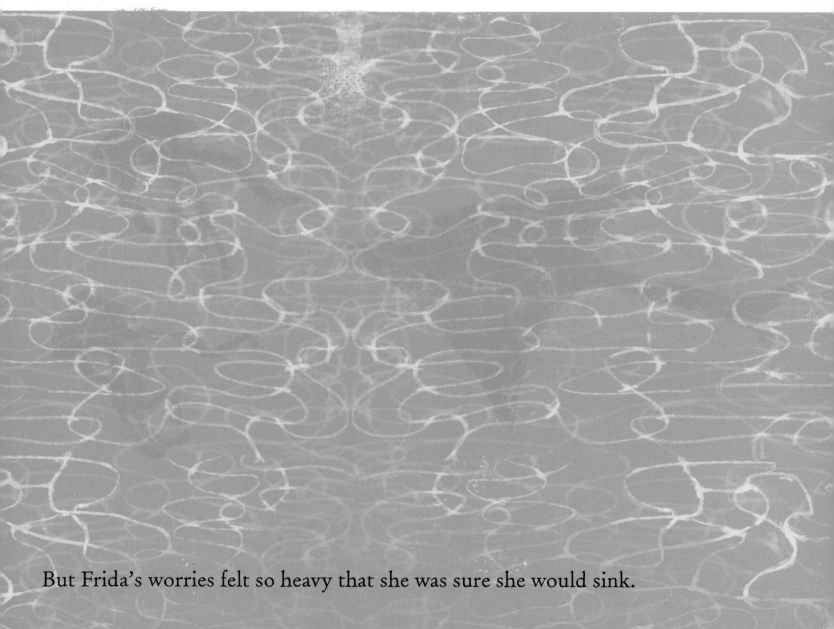

But Frida's worries felt so heavy that she was sure she would sink.

Some days her worries became
the only thing that Frida could
think about, and they weighed
her down, just like the pebbles
in her pockets.

Sundays were different though. Sunday was Frida's favourite day because Granny always came over.

Granny was funny and kind
and she gave the best hugs.

But this week Frida was
worried that even one of
Granny's hugs might not
make her feel better.

'Let's make jam, today, Frida!' said Granny.

Frida smiled. She loved cooking.

'You know, everybody has worries,' said Granny as they tossed strawberries into a huge pan together, 'even me! And worrying about them makes them worse.'

But Frida didn't know how to stop worrying about her worries.

Frida and Granny made lots and lots of jam, and when they were finished, Granny pulled a big empty jar out of her bag.

'I've had an idea to help you with your worries,' she said. 'You could put your worry pebbles into this jar so that they don't weigh you down any more.'

Frida jiggled the heavy pebbles in her pockets
and thought about what Granny had said.

Then, carefully, she put the pebbles into her jar
– one by one – all except her special pebble.

A pebble for every worry.

Soon, the jar was full, but Frida was worried that
it wasn't going to make her worries go away.

'Look, the sun's just come out, Frida!'
said Granny. 'Let's go to the park.'

Frida thought about her wellies.
She thought about her sunhat.

She decided to wear both, just in case.

'I'm going to wear my sunhat,' said Granny.

Frida nodded and smiled
and put her wellies back.

At the park, she swung on the swings, higher and higher.

She slid
down
the slide
and
laughed
out loud.

It was fast!
But she wasn't worried!

On the way home, a pebble
glinted in the sunshine.

Frida stopped and looked,
but she didn't pick it up.

That week,
Milo came over
to Frida's house.

'What's for tea?' he asked.

'It's fish fingers and chips,' Frida replied.
'Oh, and some peas too!'

On Saturday, at swim club, Frida hesitated at the edge of the pool.

'Jump, Frida!' called Milo.

Frida thought about her worries and all of her pebbles safe in the jar.

Then she took a **big jump.**

And guess what?

She didn't sink!

'I can swim like a fish!'
she laughed.

That night, at bedtime, Rabbit
had reappeared!

Frida gave him a cuddle, then she reached under
the pillow and found her special pebble. The last one.

She held it in her hand and then gently
put it on the top of the pebbles in the jar,
before tightly closing the lid.

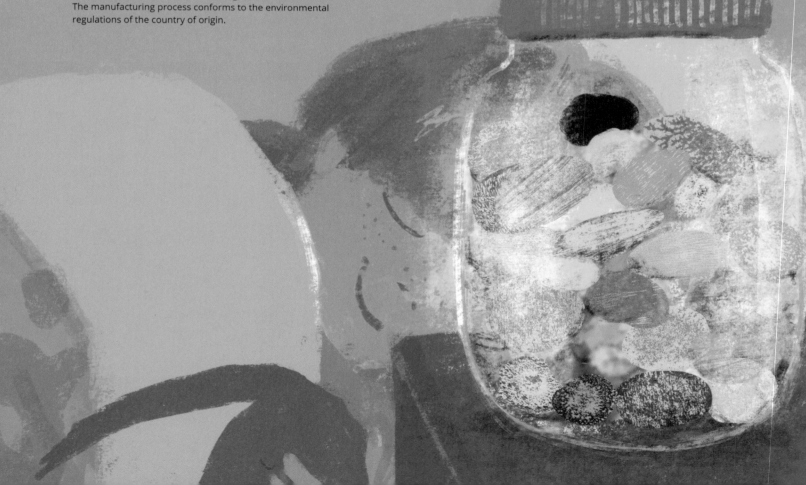

UNIVERSITY PRESS

Great Clarendon Street, Oxford OX2 6DP
Oxford University Press is a department of the University of Oxford.
It furthers the University's objective of excellence in research, scholarship,
and education by publishing worldwide. Oxford is a registered trade mark
of Oxford University Press in the UK and in certain other countries

Text copyright © Lou John 2022
Illustrations copyright © Jenny Bloomfield 2022

The moral rights of the author have been asserted

Database right Oxford University Press (maker)

First published in 2022

British Library Cataloguing in Publication Data

Data available

ISBN: 978-0-19-278273-1

10 9 8 7 6 5 4 3 2 1

Printed in China

Paper used in the production of this book is a natural,
recyclable product made from wood grown in sustainable forests.
The manufacturing process conforms to the environmental
regulations of the country of origin.

For my Amelia
- L.J.

To my husband, Dave
- J.B.